Brian
First
Publishing

The Lost Birdie and the Hungry Cat.

Mother bird sets out early in the day to look for food. She tells Little Birdie to stay put till she gets back. Their nest is in the woods near a city.

Little Birdie is too curious to just wait. He wants to try out his wings. It is hard at first with just one lesson yesterday. But then it gets easier as he spreads his wings. But wait, where is Mommy? Suddenly Little Birdie realizes he is no longer in the woods. He is lost. As he wanders around the city alley, he meets up with a hungry cat.

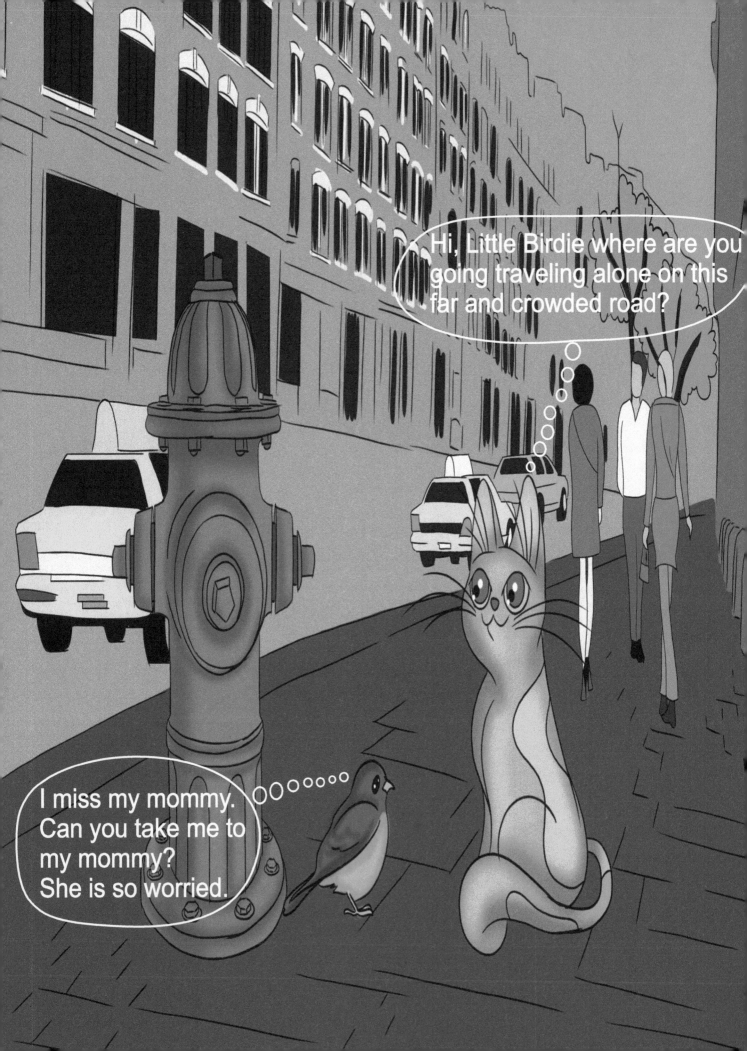

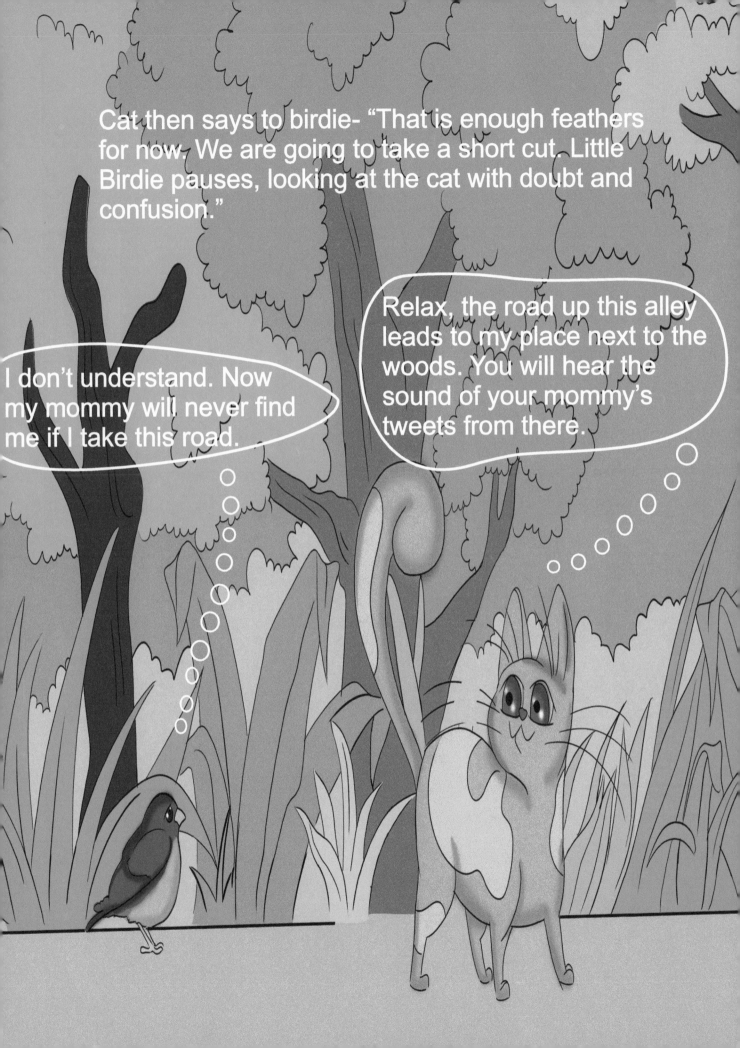

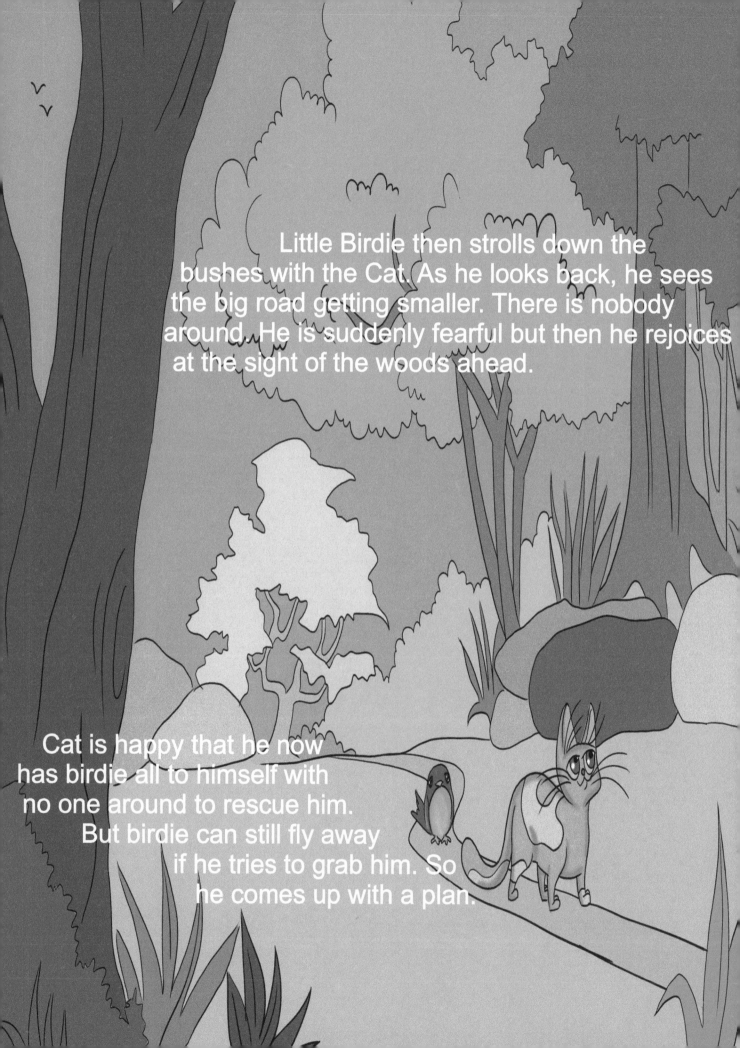

Little Birdie then strolls down the bushes with the Cat. As he looks back, he sees the big road getting smaller. There is nobody around. He is suddenly fearful but then he rejoices at the sight of the woods ahead.

Cat is happy that he now has birdie all to himself with no one around to rescue him. But birdie can still fly away if he tries to grab him. So he comes up with a plan.

Cat then sets out to look for a worm for birdie to eat.

Meanwhile, birdie waits patiently for the arrival of his mommy's tweet.

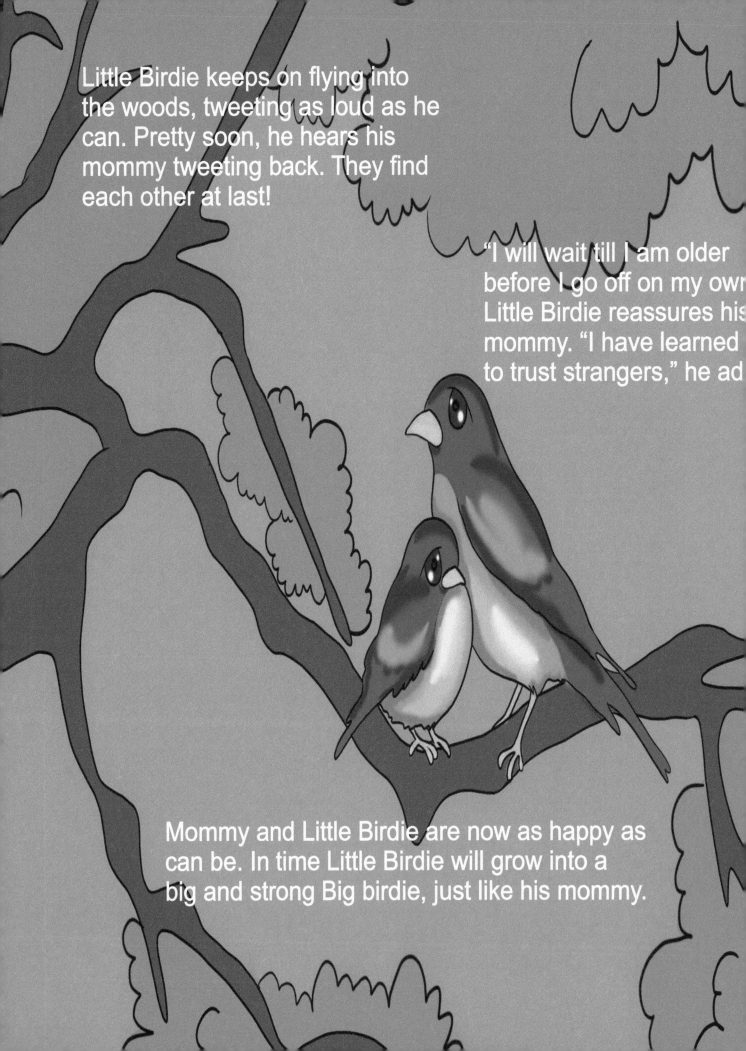

Little Birdie keeps on flying into the woods, tweeting as loud as he can. Pretty soon, he hears his mommy tweeting back. They find each other at last!

"I will wait till I am older before I go off on my own Little Birdie reassures his mommy. "I have learned to trust strangers," he ad

Mommy and Little Birdie are now as happy as can be. In time Little Birdie will grow into a big and strong Big birdie, just like his mommy.

Watch out

for

"Little birdie learns to fly"

and

"Freedom", The wolf with a big heart